Bravo Phonics

Cecilia Chan

U0108479

Level 5

The Commercial Press

Edited by: Betty Wong

Cover designed by: Cathy Chiu

Typeset by: Rong Zhou

Printing arranged by: Kenneth Lung

Bravo Phonics (Level 5)

Author: Cecilia Chan

Publisher: The Commercial Press (H.K.) Ltd.

8/F, Eastern Central Plaza, 3 Yiu Hing Road, Shau Kei Wan, H.K.

http://www.commercialpress.com.hk

Distributor: THE SUP Publishing Logistics (H.K.) Ltd.

16/F, Tsuen Wan Industrial Building, 220-248 Texaco Road,

Tsuen Wan, NT, Hong Kong

Printer: Elegance Printing and Book Binding Co., Ltd.

Block A, 4/F, Hoi Bun Industrial Building 6 Wing Yip Street,

Kwun Tung Kowloon, Hong Kong

© 2023 The Commercial Press (H.K.) Ltd.

First edition, First printing, July 2023

ISBN 978 962 07 0624 0

Printed in Hong Kong

Bravo Phonics Series is a special gift to all children - the ability to READ ENGLISH accurately and fluently!

ENJOY!

About the Author

The author, Ms Cecilia Chan, is a well-known English educator with many years of teaching experience. Passionate and experienced in teaching English, Ms Chan has taught students from over 30 schools in Hong Kong, including Marymount Primary School, Marymount Secondary School, Diocesan Boys' School, Diocesan Girls' School, St. Paul's Co-educational College, St. Paul's Co-educational College Primary School, St. Paul's College, St. Paul's Convent School (Primary and Secondary Sections), Belilios Public School, Raimondi College Primary Section, St. Clare's Primary School, St. Joseph's Primary School, St. Joseph's College, Pun U Association Wah Yan Primary School and other international schools. Many of Ms Chan's students have won prizes in Solo Verse Speaking, Prose Reading and Public Speaking at the Hong Kong Schools Speech Festival and

other interschool open speech contests. Driven
by her passion in promoting English learning,
Ms Chan has launched the Bravo Phonics Series
(Levels 1-5) as an effective tool to foster a
love of English reading and learning in children.

To all my Beloved Students

Acknowledgement

Many thanks to the Editor, JY Ho, for her effort and contribution to the editing of the Bravo Phonics Series and her assistance all along.

Author's Words

The fundamental objective of phonics teaching is to develop step-by-step a child's ability to pronounce and recognize the words in the English language. Each phonic activity is a means to build up the child's power of word recognition until such power has been thoroughly exercised that word recognition becomes practically automatic.

Proper phonic training is highly important to young children especially those with English as a second language. It enables a child to acquire a large reading vocabulary in a comparatively short time and hence can happily enjoy fluent story reading. By giving phonics a place in the daily allotment of children's activities, they can be brought to a state of reading proficiency at an early age. Be patient, allow ample time for children to enjoy each and every phonic activity; if it is well and truly done, further steps will be taken easily and much more quickly.

Bravo Phonics Series has proven to be of value in helping young children reach the above objective and embark joyfully on the voyage of learning to read. It consists of five books of five levels, covering all the letter sounds of the consonants,

short and long vowels, diphthongs and blends in the English language. Bravo Phonics Series employs a step-by-step approach, integrating different learning skills through a variety of fun reading, writing, drawing, spelling and story-telling activities. There are quizzes, drills, tongue twisters, riddles and comprehension exercises to help consolidate all the letter sounds learnt. The QR code on each page enables a child to self-learn at home by following the instructions of Ms Chan while simultaneously practising the letter sounds through the example given.

The reward to teachers and parents will be a thousandfold when children gain self-confidence and begin to apply their phonic experiences to happy story reading.

Contents

Quick Guide

 Read

 Write

 Scan

 Colour

 Circle

 Draw

Answer Key

 **Say**

 **Spell**

 **Check**

 Cross Out

 Join

Hello, this is Ms Chan. How are you?
Are you ready to learn Bravo Phonics?
Let's begin!

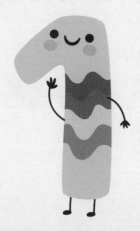

Comprehensions

Comprehension 1

 Listen to the reading.

 Complete the sentences.

The Cat

Candy has a cat.
It is her very
best friend.

1 _____ has a cat.

2 Candy _____ a cat.

3 Candy has a _____ .

4 It is _____ very best friend.

5 It is her _____ best

_____
_____ .

6 Candy _____ a _____ .

_____ is _____ very

_____ friend.

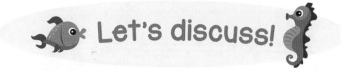 Let's discuss!

1 Do you have a cat?

2 Is it your very best friend?

3 What kind of a pet would you like to have?

A dog?   A turtle?

A rabbit?   A bird?

A _____

Listen to the reading.

 Complete the sentences.

The Puppy

Dave has a puppy.
It is his beloved
pet.

1 _____ has a puppy.

2 Dave _____ a puppy.

3 Dave has a _____ .

4 It is _____ beloved pet.

4

5 It is his beloved _____ .

6 Dave _____ a _____ .

   _____ is his _____

   _____ .

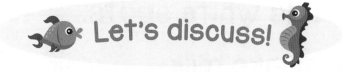

Let's discuss!

1 Do you have a puppy?

2 Is it your beloved pet?

3 How do you take care of your pet?

Comprehension 3

 Listen to the reading.

 Answer the questions in complete sentences.

My Kitten

My kitten is orange.

She has white spots.

She drinks milk.

She eats cat food.

1 What colour is my kitten?

2 What colour are her spots?

3 What does she drink?

4 What does she eat?

 Let's check the answers.

Now draw the kitten.

 Be sure to colour her orange with white spots!

Listen to the reading.

 Answer the questions in complete sentences.

The Duck

Here is a white duck.

Her beak is yellow.

She likes to swim.

She lives in the pond.

1 What colour is the duck?

....

_____

2 What colour is her beak?

....

_____

3 What does she like to do?

....

_____

4 Where does she live?

....

_____

 Let's check the answers.

11

Let's think!

Where can you see ducks in Hong Kong?

In the parks?

 Now draw two ducks swimming in the pond.

 Colour the picture.

Listen to the reading.

 Answer the questions in complete sentences.

The Octopus

Here comes the octopus!

It is pink in colour.

It has eight long legs.

It lives in the sea.

It eats crabs and clams for food.

1 What colour is the octopus?

_____

_____

2 How many legs has the octopus?

_____

_____

_____

_____

3 Where does it live?

_____

_____

4 What does it eat for food?

_____

_____

_____

_____

 Let's check the answers.

15

16

Draw an octopus swimming in the sea.

 Colour the picture.

17

Comprehension 6

 Listen to the reading.

 Answer the questions in complete sentences.

Lambs

Lambs give us wool.

They are white in colour.

Wool is cut off from lambs.

The wool is cut in spring.

Clothes are made from wool.

1   What give us wool?

_____

_____

2   What is cut off from lambs?

_____

_____

_____

3   When is the wool cut?

_____

_____

_____

4   What are made from wool?

_____

_____

_____

 Let's check the answers.

Let's think!

Why do we cut the lambs' wool in spring?

Why not in winter?

 Now draw two lambs. One has its wool cut off!

 Colour the picture.

21

Listen to the reading.

 Answer the questions in complete sentences.

My Ears

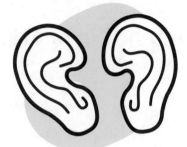

I have two ears.

I can hear a dog bark.

I can hear a cat mew.

I can hear a bird singing in the tree.

I can hear a little baby crying loudly.

My ears help me hear sounds.

1 What will bark?

....

_____

2 What will mew?

....

_____

3 Where is the bird?

....

_____

4 What is the bird doing?

....

_____

5 Who is little?

....

_____

6 What is the baby doing?

....

_____

7 What help you hear?

....

_____

 Let's check the answers.

23

Comprehension 8
Using your Senses

 Write the number in the box that completes each sentence.

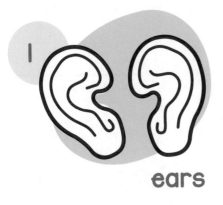

1

ears

2

hands

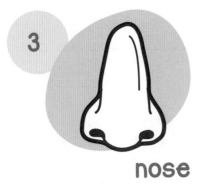

3

nose

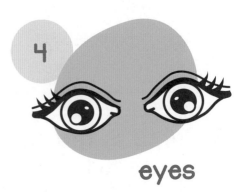

4

eyes

5

tongue

24

1   I see with my ☐ .

2   I hear with my ☐ .

3   I taste with my ☐ .

4   I smell with my ☐ .

5   I touch with my ☐ .

 Let's check the answers.

Comprehension 9
How do you know?

Write the number in the box that completes each sentence.

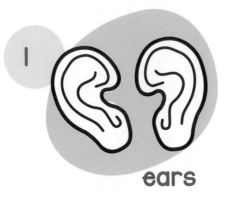

1

ears

2

hands

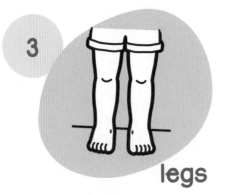

3

legs

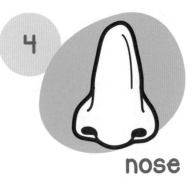

4

nose

5

eyes

6

tongue

1   The stove is hot.   ☐

2   The flowers are red.   ☐

3   The food is nice.   ☐

4   The skunk is here.   ☐

5   The children are singing.   ☐

6   The boys can play soccer.   ☐

 Let's check the answers.

Comprehension 10
How do you feel?

 Write the number in the box that completes each sentence.

1   angry

2   happy

3   hot and tired

4   sad

5   puzzled

6   sleepy

1   You ran for half an hour.   ☐

2   Your best friend doesn't talk to you.   ☐

3   Your brother made fun of you.   ☐

4   You went to bed too late.   ☐

5   You got a new toy for your birthday.   ☐

6   You can't figure out the riddle.   ☐

 Let's check the answers.

Listen to the reading.

 Complete the sentences.

Could this be true?

We see, we hear and we learn things.

Some things are true.

Some things are clear.

Some things are not true.

Some things are queer.

Can you tell which is which?

We _____ , we _____

and we _____ things.

Some things are _____ .

Some _____ are _____ .

_____ _____ are not true.

Some things are _____ .

Can you tell _____ is

_____ ?

31

Put the right face on the line.

 true

 not true

1 _____ My baby brother is as

big as a lion.

2 _____ A chair is to sit on.

3 _____ A mother dog has

puppies.

4 _____ A lamb can fly up to

the sky.

5 _____ A house is as small as a mouse.

6 _____ The sun is very bright.

7 _____ A turtle can walk as fast as a rabbit.

 Let's check the answers.

Listen to the reading.

The Queer House

This is a queer house.

It is not very far from my house.

I see it every day.

I call it the queer house.

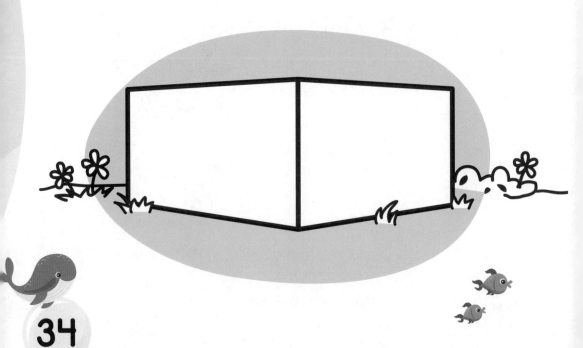

1   Why do I call it the queer house?

 Draw a line from each sentence to the right picture.

It has no roof.   •

It has no door.   •

It has no windows.   •

2 Can you fix it?

Put a roof on the house.

Put a door in the house.

Put two windows in the house.

3 Can you make it pretty?

Colour the roof red.

Colour the door brown.

Colour the walls yellow.

Do not colour the windows!

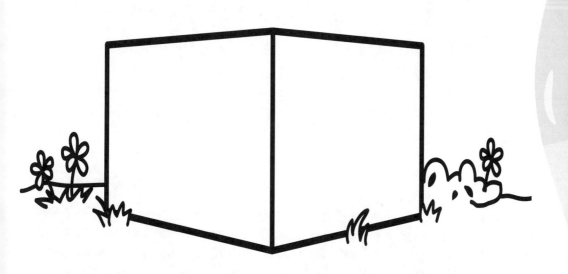

Comprehension 13

 Say the names of the animals after me.

camel

giraffe

zebra

horse

Say the different parts of the lion after me.

eye   nose   ear   body

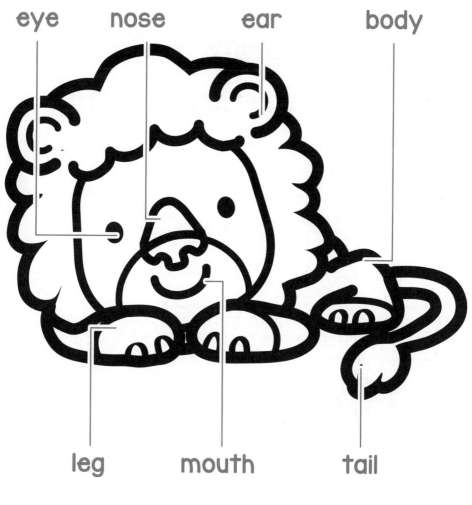

leg   mouth   tail

lion

What's this?

 Look at the picture and guess what the part of the body belongs to.

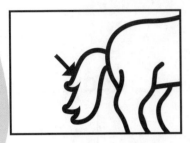 What's this?

It's the horse's tail.

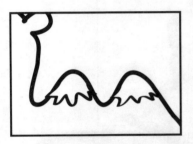 What's this?

 What's this?

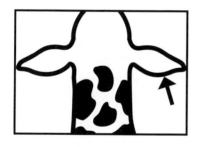

What's this?

....

_____

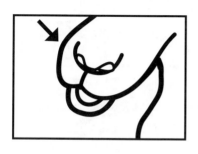

What's this?

....

_____

What's this?

....

_____

 Let's check the answers.

Have you got a good memory?

Look carefully at the picture. Try to remember everything.

Now cover the picture with a book.

 Write down the number of the following animals and birds.

_____ dogs

_____ mice

_____ birds

_____ owls

_____ pigs

_____ crocodiles

_____ snakes

 Let's check the answers.

43

Have you tried Tongue Twisters before? They are great fun!

Tongue Twisters

'**s**' and '**f**'

'**h**' and '**t**'

'**p**' and '**m**'

'**n**' and '**r**'

'**b**' and '**c**'

'**d**' and '**l**'

Tongue Twisters 's' and 'f'

Look at the pictures and read the tongue twisters after me.

Underline all the words with the beginning sound 's' in number I and all the words with the beginning sound 'f' in number 2.

I Sing a song, singing along with sweet Suzie and Susan.

46

2 Feel the feathers fly, flying freely in the sky.

 Let's check the answers.

 Now colour the pictures.

Tongue Twisters
'h' and 't'

Look at the pictures and read the tongue twisters after me.

Underline all the words with the beginning sound 'h' in number 3 and all the words with the beginning sound 't' in number 4.

3 Hungry Henry is gobbling up the huge hamburger in a hurry.

4 Ten tiny tweeties trembling on the tree top.

 Let's check the answers.

 Now colour the pictures.

Tongue Twisters
'p' and 'm'

 Look at the pictures and read the tongue twisters after me.

Underline all the words with the beginning sound 'p' in number 5 and all the words with the beginning sound 'm' in number 6.

5   Polly and Patty are playing with their pretty puffy pet.

6 Mummy is making many muffins for Mable and Mark.

 Let's check the answers.

 Now colour the pictures.

51

Tongue Twisters 'n' and 'r'

 Look at the pictures and read the tongue twisters after me.

Underline all the words with the beginning sound 'n' in number 7 and all the words with the beginning sound 'r' in number 8.

7 Naughty Nick is jumping on Nelly's nice neat bed.

8 Row, row, rowing the red boat in the rain.

 Let's check the answers.

 Now colour the pictures.

Tongue Twisters 'b' and 'c'

 Look at the pictures and read the tongue twisters after me.

Underline all the words with the beginning sound 'b' in number 9 and all the words with the beginning sound 'c' in number 10.

9 Bobby blows up the balloon and Betty bounces the big ball.

10 Candy is catching the cap that falls from the clothes closet.

 Let's check the answers.

 Now colour the pictures.

Tongue Twisters
'd' and 'l'

Look at the pictures and read the tongue twisters after me.

Underline all the words with the beginning sound 'd' in number 11 and all the words with the beginning sound 'l' in number 12.

11 Daddy is beating the drum while Daisy is dancing with the doggie.

12 Little Lily loves to lie lazily on the laptop.

 Let's check the answers.

 Now colour the pictures.

Let's have some Fun with Spellings!

Fun with Spellings

'i'
'ai'
'ee'
'oa'
'ue'
'age'
'qu'

Magic 'e'
Silent 'h'
Silent 'b'
Silent 'k'

Fun with Spellings
'i' words

The following words all contain the letter 'i' that sounds like the letter 'i'.

Use the clues and pictures to complete the spellings.

 Listen to the clues.

1 i ☐ ☐ ☐

2 ☐ i ☐ ☐ ☐

3 ☐ ☐ i ☐ ☐ ☐

4 ☐ i ☐ ☐ ☐

5 i ☐ ☐ ☐

1   a common metal from which steel is made

2   coming at the end

3   screens for windows to keep off light

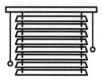

4   a huge figure or monster

5   having nothing to do; carefree

 Let's check the answers and read after me.

Can you think of other words with 'i' that sound like the letter 'i' ?

_____   _____

_____   _____

Fun with Spellings
'ai' words

The following words all contain the letter 'ai' that sound like the letter 'a'.

Use the clues and pictures to complete the spellings.

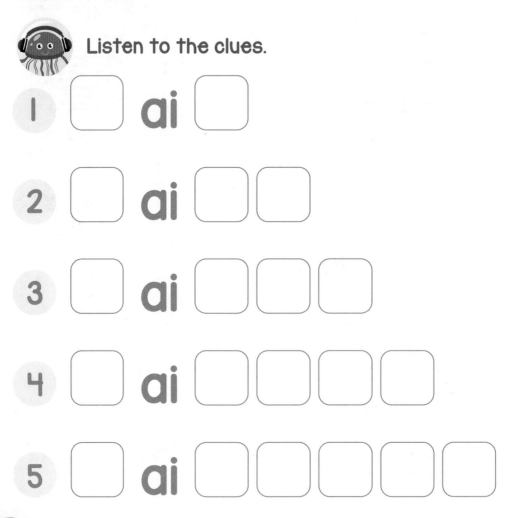

Listen to the clues.

1 ☐ **ai** ☐

2 ☐ **ai** ☐ ☐

3 ☐ **ai** ☐ ☐ ☐

4 ☐ **ai** ☐ ☐ ☐ ☐

5 ☐ **ai** ☐ ☐ ☐ ☐ ☐

1   it falls from the sky; plants need it

2   to make a picture with colours

3   a person who works on a ship

4   people who make clothes

5   being loyal; keeping promises

 Let's check the answers and read after me.

Can you think of other words with 'ai' that sound like the letter 'a'?

_____ _____

_____ _____

Fun with Spellings
'ee' words

The following words all contain the letters 'ee'. that sound like the letter 'e'.

Use the clues and pictures to complete the spellings.

 Listen to the clues.

1   ee ☐

2   ☐ ee ☐

3   ☐ ☐ ee ☐

4   ☐ ☐ ☐ ee ☐

5   ☐ ☐ ☐ ☐ ee ☐

1 a snake-like fish

2 insects with stings at the end of their bodies

3 a very strong and light metal made from iron

4 a flat surface on which pictures and words are shown

5 a unit to show the temperature of a place

 Let's check the answers and read after me.

Can you think of other words with 'ee' that sound like the letter 'e'?

_____   _____

_____   _____

65

Fun with Spellings
'oa' words

The following words all contain the letters 'oa' that sound like the letter 'o'.

Use the clues and pictures to complete the spellings.

 Listen to the clues.

1  oa

2  oa

3 oa

4  oa

5  oa

66

1   a frog-like animal which lives both in water and on land

2   a very young horse

3   something in which people can travel across water

4   does not sink in water

5   how your tummy feels after eating too much

 Let's check the answers and read after me.

Can you think of other words with 'oa' that sound like the letter 'o'?

_____   _____

_____   _____

Fun with Spellings
'ue' words

The following words all contain the letters 'ue' that sound like the letter 'u'.

Use the clues and pictures to complete the spellings.

 Listen to the clues.

1 ☐ ☐ ue

2 ☐ ☐ ue

3 ☐ ☐ ue

4 ☐ ☐ ☐ ue

5 ☐ ☐ ☐ ue

1   a fact or idea that helps to solve a problem

2   a substance used for sticking materials together

3   something accurate or exact

4   give reasons in support of an idea or quarrel

5   regard something to be useful, worthy or important

 Let's check the answers and read after me.

Can you think of other words with 'ue' that sound like the letter 'u'?

_____ _____

_____ _____

Fun with Spellings
'age' words

The following words all end with the letters 'age' that sound like the letter 'h'.

Use the clues and pictures to complete the spellings.

 Listen to the clues.

1 ☐ age

2 ☐ ☐ age

3 ☐ ☐ ☐ age

4 ☐ ☐ ☐ ☐ age

5 ☐ ☐ ☐ ☐ ☐ age

1 anger

2 a platform where people perform

3 a journey on the sea

4 from thirteen to nineteen years old

5 two people getting married

 Let's check the answers and read after me.

Can you think of other words with 'age' that sound like the letter 'h'?

_____   _____

_____   _____

71

Fun with Spellings
'qu' words

The following words all start with the letters 'qu' that sound like 'kw'.

Use the clues and pictures to complete the spellings.

 Listen to the clues.

1 q u ☐ ☐

2 q u ☐ ☐ ☐

3 q u ☐ ☐ ☐ ☐

4 q u ☐ ☐ ☐ ☐ ☐

5 q u ☐ ☐ ☐ ☐ ☐ ☐

72

1   a short test with a set of questions to be answered

2   with little noise

3   to shiver or tremble

4   one fourth of a whole

5   to ask or to seek for an answer

 Let's check the answers and read after me.

Can you think of other words with 'qu' that sound like 'kw'?

_____ _____

_____ _____

73

Fun with Spellings
Magic 'e'

Adding the silent 'e' to the end of a word can change the vowel sound in front — short 'a' sound becomes the long 'a' sound.

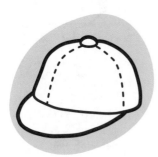

cap + 'e' =

tap + 'e' =

hat + 'e' = ☐ ☐ ☐ ☐

can + 'e' = ☐ ☐ ☐ ☐

man + 'e' = ☐ ☐ ☐ ☐

 Let's check the answers.

Fun with Spellings
Magic 'e'

Adding the silent 'e' to the end of a word can change the vowel sound in front — short 'i' sound becomes the long 'i' sound.

dim + 'e' =

fin + 'e' =

pin + 'e' = ▢ ▢ ▢ ▢

rip + 'e' = ▢ ▢ ▢ ▢

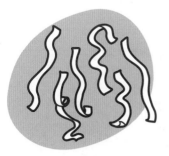 

strip + 'e' = ▢ ▢ ▢ ▢ ▢ ▢

 Let's check the answers.

Fun with Spellings
Magic 'e'

Adding the silent 'e' to the end of a word can change the vowel sound in front — short 'o' sound becomes the long 'o' sound.

B20065028

cod + 'e' = ☐ ☐ ☐ ☐

dot + 'e' = ☐ ☐ ☐ ☐

hop + 'e' =

not + 'e' =

rob + 'e' =

 Let's check the answers.

Fun with Spellings
Magic 'e'

Adding the silent 'e' to the end of a word can change the vowel sound in front — short 'u' sound becomes the long 'u' sound.

cut + 'e' = ☐☐☐☐

tub + 'e' = ☐☐☐☐

80

run + 'e' = ⬜ ⬜ ⬜ ⬜

dun + 'e' = ⬜ ⬜ ⬜ ⬜

 Let's check the answers.

Fun with Spellings
Silent 'h'

The following words all contain the silent 'h'.

Use the clues and pictures to complete the spellings.

 Listen to the clues.

1 ⬜ h ⬜ ⬜ ⬜ ⬜

2 ⬜ h ⬜ ⬜ ⬜ ⬜

3 ⬜ h ⬜ ⬜ ⬜ ⬜

4 h ⬜ ⬜ ⬜ ⬜ ⬜

1   Large animals with thick grey skin and horns on their noses

2   Short poems with rhyming words at the end of their lines

3   Circular objects that enable a car to move along the ground

4   Always telling the truth

 Let's check the answers and read after me.

Can you think of other words with the silent 'h'?

_____   _____

_____   _____

83

Fun with Spellings
Silent 'b'

The following words all contain the silent 'b'.

Use the clues and pictures to complete the spellings.

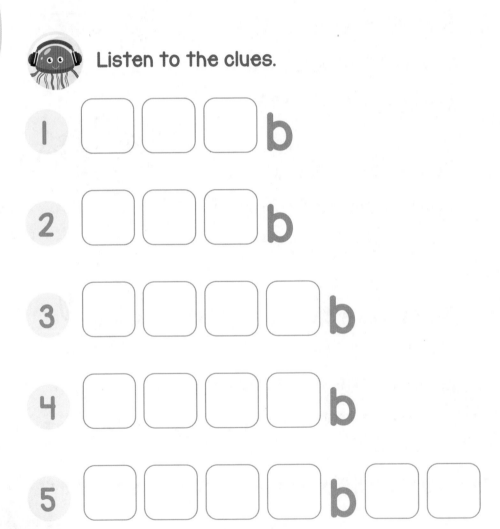

Listen to the clues.

1. ☐☐☐ b

2. ☐☐☐ b

3. ☐☐☐☐ b

4. ☐☐☐☐ b

5. ☐☐☐☐ b ☐☐

84

1   Something which explodes and destroys a large area

2   Part of a woman's body where a baby grows before it is born

3   The act of moving towards the top of something

4   The first finger of your hand

5   A person who fixes and repairs pipes

 Let's check the answers and read after me.

Can you think of other words with the silent 'b'?

_____   _____

_____   _____

85

Fun with Spellings
Silent 'k'

The following words all contain the silent 'k'.

Use the clues and pictures to complete the spellings.

 Listen to the clues.

1 k ☐☐☐

2 k ☐☐☐

3 k ☐☐☐☐

4 k ☐☐☐☐

5 k ☐☐☐☐

1 A round handle on a door or drawer for opening or closing it

2 Make something from wool by using two needles or machine

3 A tool for cutting things

4 Hit on a surface especially on the door or table

5 To bend one's legs so that the knees are touching the ground

 Let's check the answers and read after me.

Can you think of other words with the silent 'k'?

_____   _____

_____   _____

Are you ready for more practice?
Let's begin!

Minimal Pairs

Minimal Pairs

 Read the sentences.

 Tick the sentence that matches the picture.

She wants a <u>b</u>ug.

She wants a <u>h</u>ug.

He is enjoying the <u>s</u>un.

He is enjoying the <u>b</u>un.

I got a <u>k</u>ite.

I got a <u>b</u>ite.

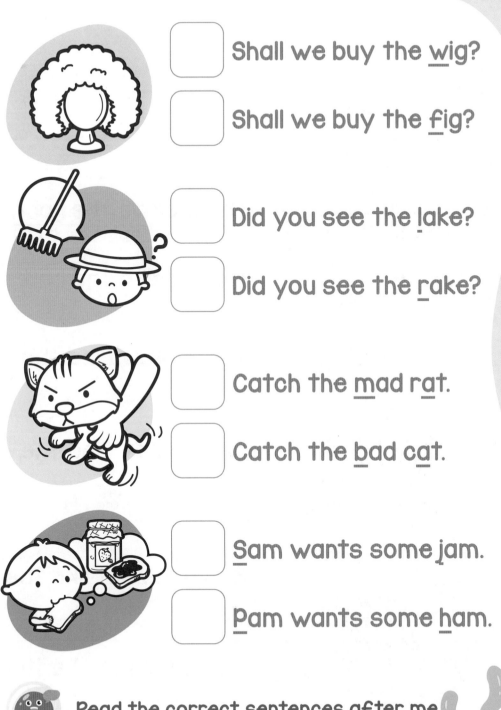

☐ Shall we buy the <u>w</u>ig?

☐ Shall we buy the <u>f</u>ig?

☐ Did you see the <u>l</u>ake?

☐ Did you see the <u>r</u>ake?

☐ Catch the <u>m</u>ad r<u>a</u>t.

☐ Catch the <u>b</u>ad c<u>a</u>t.

☐ <u>S</u>am wants some jam.

☐ <u>P</u>am wants some <u>h</u>am.

 Read the correct sentences after me.

 Now colour the pictures.

91

Minimal Pairs

 Read the sentences.

 Tick the sentence that matches the picture.

He goes to the roo<u>m</u>.

He goes to the roo<u>f</u>.

We cannot find the bu<u>s</u>.

We cannot find the bu<u>d</u>.

She does not like the fo<u>x</u>.

She does not like the fo<u>g</u>.

92

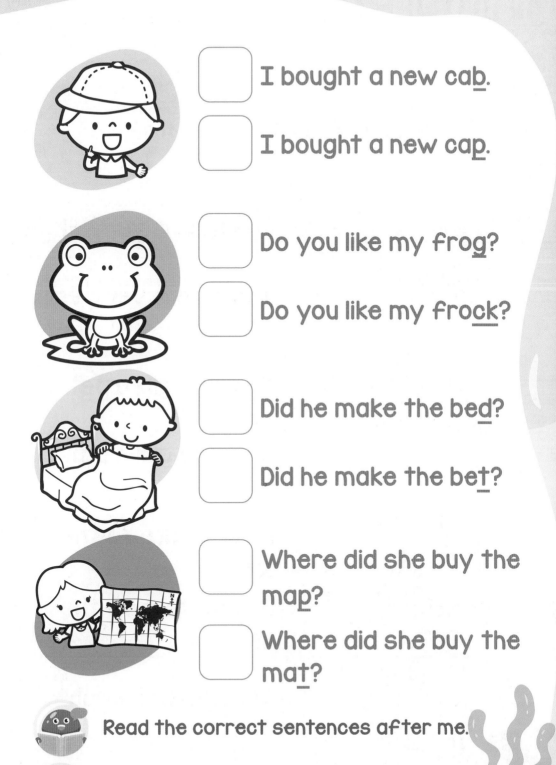

I bought a new ca<u>b</u>.

I bought a new ca<u>p</u>.

Do you like my fro<u>g</u>?

Do you like my fro<u>ck</u>?

Did he make the be<u>d</u>?

Did he make the be<u>t</u>?

Where did she buy the ma<u>p</u>?

Where did she buy the ma<u>t</u>?

Read the correct sentences after me.

Now colour the pictures.

93

Minimal Pairs

 Read the sentences.

 Tick the sentence that matches the picture.

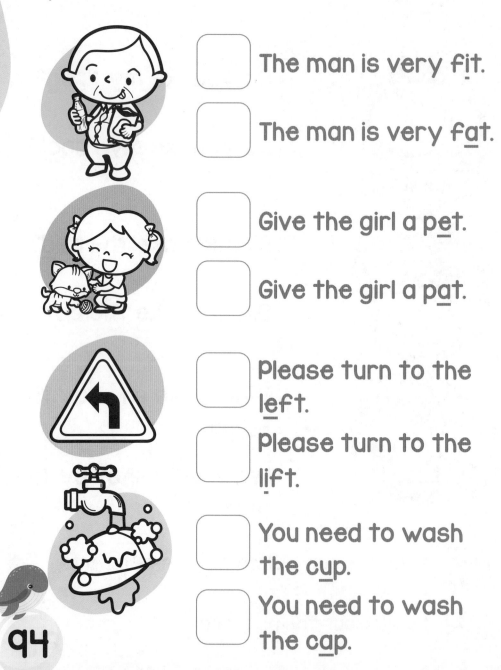

The man is very f<u>i</u>t.

The man is very f<u>a</u>t.

Give the girl a p<u>e</u>t.

Give the girl a p<u>a</u>t.

Please turn to the l<u>e</u>ft.

Please turn to the l<u>i</u>ft.

You need to wash the c<u>u</u>p.

You need to wash the c<u>a</u>p.

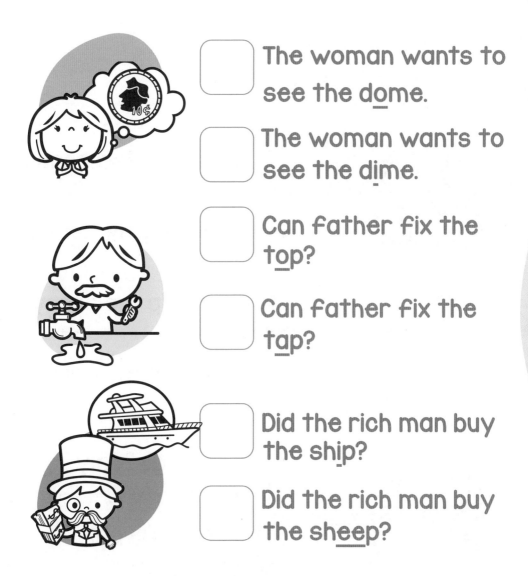

☐ The woman wants to see the d<u>o</u>me.

☐ The woman wants to see the d<u>i</u>me.

☐ Can father fix the t<u>o</u>p?

☐ Can father fix the t<u>a</u>p?

☐ Did the rich man buy the sh<u>i</u>p?

☐ Did the rich man buy the sh<u>ee</u>p?

 Read the correct sentences after me.

 Now colour the pictures.

Minimal Pairs

 Read the sentences.

 Tick the sentence that matches the picture.

Don't sit on the grass.

Don't sit on the glass.

Please help me carry the rock.

Please help me carry the clock.

The little girl only wants to play.

The little girl only wants to pray.

The child is trying to think.

The child is trying to blink.

96

☐ Father will buy it for <u>m</u>other.

☐ Father will buy it for <u>br</u>other.

☐ The boys are left in the <u>r</u>ain.

☐ The boys are left in the <u>tr</u>ain.

☐ The baby loves the <u>cr</u>adle.

☐ The baby loves the <u>br</u>idle.

 Read the correct sentences after me.

 Now colour the pictures.

Minimal Pairs

 Read the sentences.

 Tick the sentence that matches the picture.

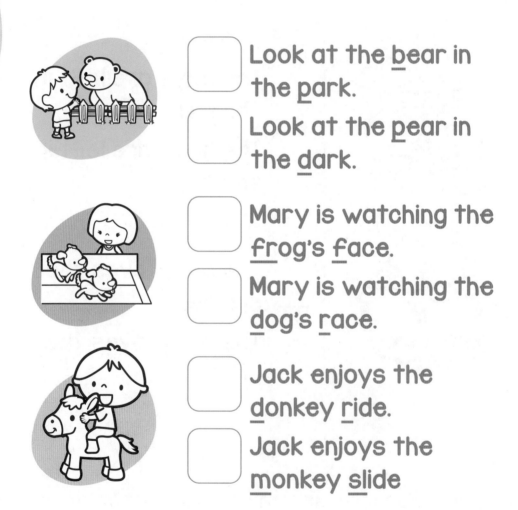

Look at the <u>b</u>ear in the <u>p</u>ark.

Look at the <u>p</u>ear in the <u>d</u>ark.

Mary is watching the <u>f</u>rog's <u>f</u>ace.

Mary is watching the <u>d</u>og's <u>r</u>ace.

Jack enjoys the <u>d</u>onkey <u>r</u>ide.

Jack enjoys the <u>m</u>onkey <u>s</u>lide

☐ The pupils are <u>s</u>inging in the <u>sch</u>ool.

☐ The pupils are <u>sw</u>inging in the <u>p</u>ool.

☐ T<u>i</u>mmy will <u>tr</u>y his <u>b</u>est.

☐ T<u>o</u>mmy will <u>dr</u>y his <u>v</u>est.

☐ <u>H</u>arry <u>fl</u>ew a <u>k</u>ite.

☐ <u>B</u>arry <u>dr</u>ew a <u>m</u>ite.

☐ Did <u>T</u>ed see the <u>t</u>all <u>m</u>an?

☐ Did <u>N</u>ed see the <u>sm</u>all <u>p</u>an?

 Read the correct sentences after me.

Now colour the pictures.

99

Minimal Pairs

 Read the sentences.

 Tick the sentence that matches the picture.

They are p<u>l</u>aying with the <u>s</u>and.

They are p<u>r</u>aying with the <u>b</u>and.

<u>B</u>arry is going to buy the <u>br</u>ight lam<u>p</u>.

<u>H</u>arry is going to buy the <u>r</u>ight lam<u>b</u>.

<u>J</u>ill loves the <u>l</u>ittle <u>m</u>ouse.

<u>B</u>ill loves the <u>br</u>ittle <u>h</u>ouse.

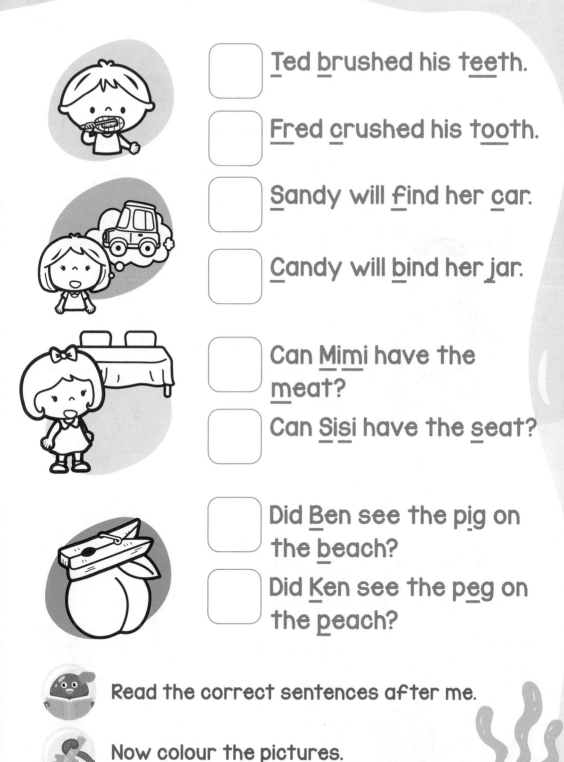

Ted brushed his teeth.

Fred crushed his tooth.

Sandy will find her car.

Candy will bind her jar.

Can Mimi have the meat?

Can Sisi have the seat?

Did Ben see the pig on the beach?

Did Ken see the peg on the peach?

Read the correct sentences after me.

Now colour the pictures.

Let's do some Riddles!
They are great fun!

Drawing and Fun Riddles

Drawing and Fun Riddles

 What am I?

 Listen to the riddles.

 Draw 'me' in the boxes.

 Make 'me' colourful.

I   The teacher writes on me with a chalk.
My face is green and I cannot talk.
Make sure you colour me green!

104

2 I can sing. I can fly. I have a beak.

 Check your answers with the answer key.

Drawing and Fun Riddles

 What am I?

 Listen to the riddles.

 Draw 'me' in the boxes.

 Make 'me' colourful.

3 My name sounds like the letter 'u'.
I am an animal. Colour me white!

4 My name sounds like the letter 'b'.
I am an insect.

5 My name sounds like the letter 't'.
I am a drink.

 Check your answers with the answer key.

Drawing and Fun Riddles

 What am I?

 Listen to the riddles.

 Draw 'me' in the boxes.

 Make 'me' colourful.

6   My first letter is in 'sun' and also in 'set'.

My second letter is both in 'lap' and 'top'.

My third and fourth letters are twins in the 'pool'.

My fifth letter is in the middle of the 'end'.

7   I have a body and a long neck but I have no legs.

8   My name sounds like the letter 'c'. I am the home of a lot of fish. Colour me blue!

 Check your answers with the answer key.

Drawing and Fun Riddles

 What am I?

 Listen to the riddle.

 Draw 'me' in the box.

 Make 'me' colourful.

9   My first letter begins in my 'hair'.

My second letter is silent in my 'toe'.

My third letter is in the middle of my 'heart' and 'ear'.

My fourth letter is at the end of my 'hand'.

 Check your answers with the answer key.

Are you ready for more challenges?
Let's start!

Wrack your Brain!

Wrack your Brain!

1   Which months have twenty-eight days in them?

_____

2   My aunt has a sister but this woman is not my aunt. Who is she?

_____

3   What do you add to a road to make it broad?

_____

4   What table has no legs?

_____

5 What hands cannot carry things?

_____

6 It stands in the middle of 'water' and appears twice in a 'turtle'. What is it?

_____

 Let's check the answers.

115

SCAN ME

7 There are two fathers and two sons. Each of them carries an umbrella but there are only three umbrellas. How can this be?

_____

_____

_____

8 There are twelve legs in the chicken farm but there are only five chickens. How can it be?

_____

_____

_____

9 There are eight boys and a basket with eight eggs in it. Each boy has one egg but one egg remains in the basket. How can it be?

_____

_____

_____

10 If you spell the word 's-t-r-e-s-s-e-d' from the end to the beginning, then miracle happens: something unhappy becomes something very sweet. What is it?

_____

 Let's check the answers.

Are you ready for more challenges?
They are great fun!

Word Pyramid

Word Pyramid

It starts off with one letter.

Add a new letter to it every time you build a new level.

No letters can be taken away but their order can be changed.

120

The vowel 'a'
Building a 3-level pyramid

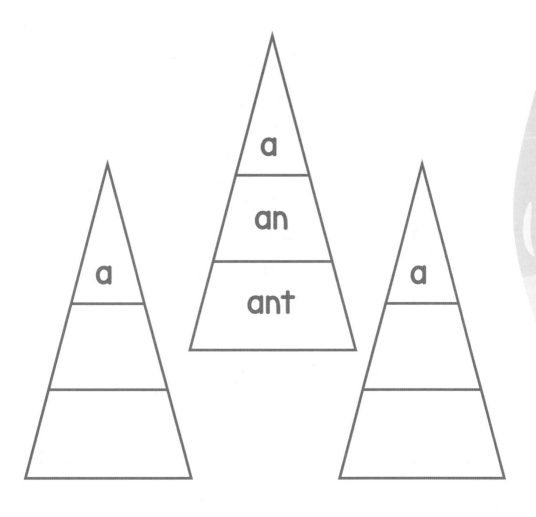

Word Pyramid

The vowel 'a'

Building a 4-level pyramid

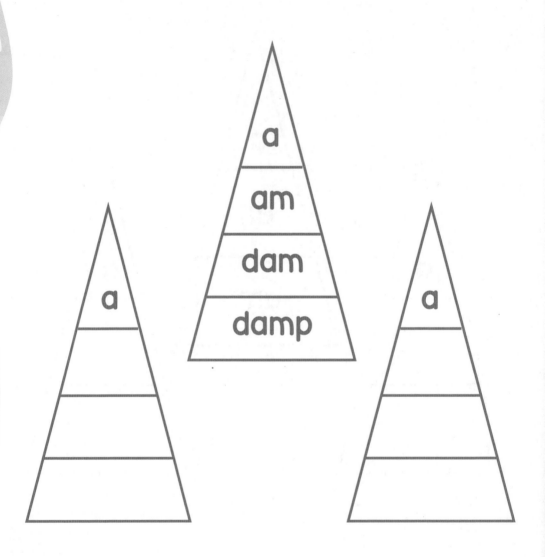

a
am
dam
damp

a

a

Building a 5-level pyramid

a
at
ate
late
plate

a

a

Word Pyramid

The vowel 'e'

Building a 3-level pyramid

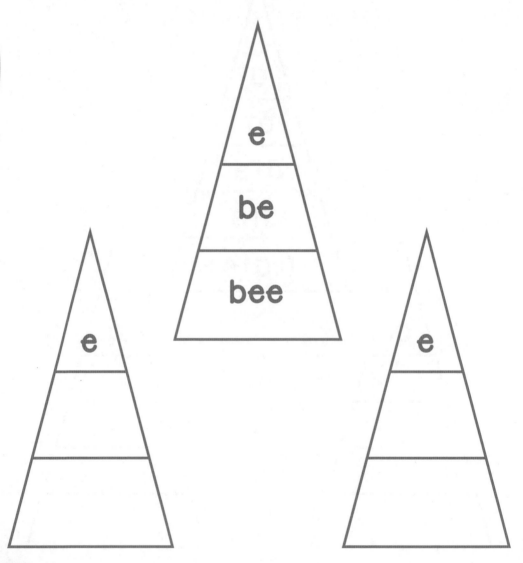

e

be

bee

e

e

The vowel 'e'
Building a 4-level pyramid

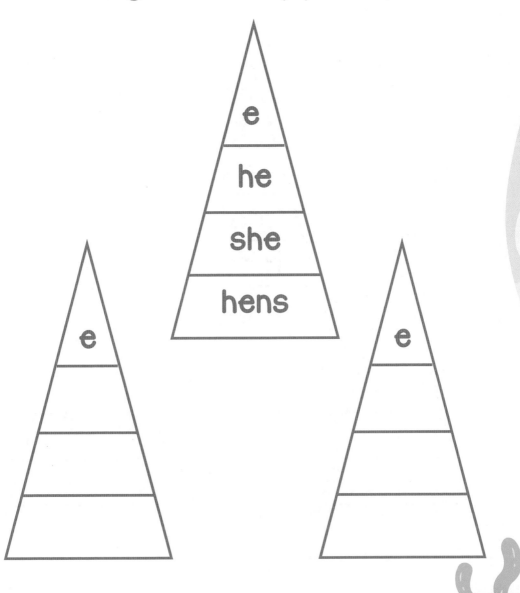

Word Pyramid

The vowel 'e'

Building a 5-level pyramid

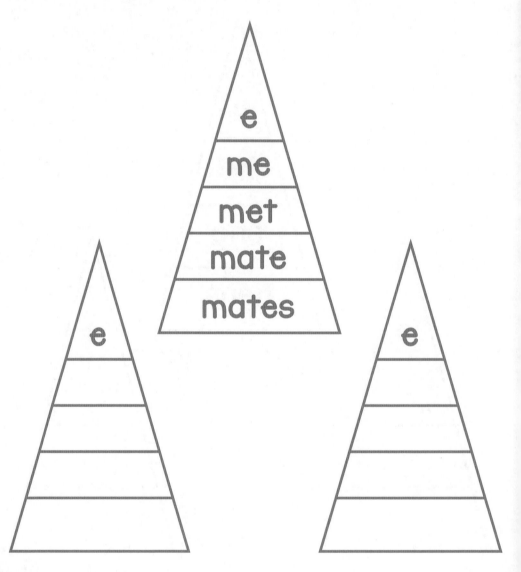

e
me
met
mate
mates

e

e

The vowel 'i'
Building a 3-level pyramid

Word Pyramid

The vowel 'i'

Building a 4-level pyramid

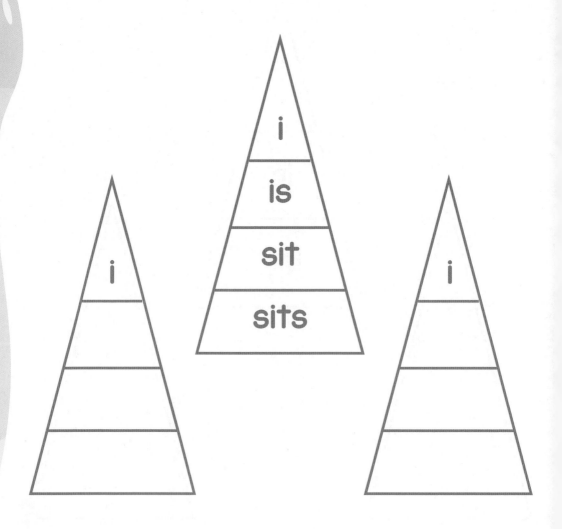

The vowel 'i'
Building a 5-level pyramid

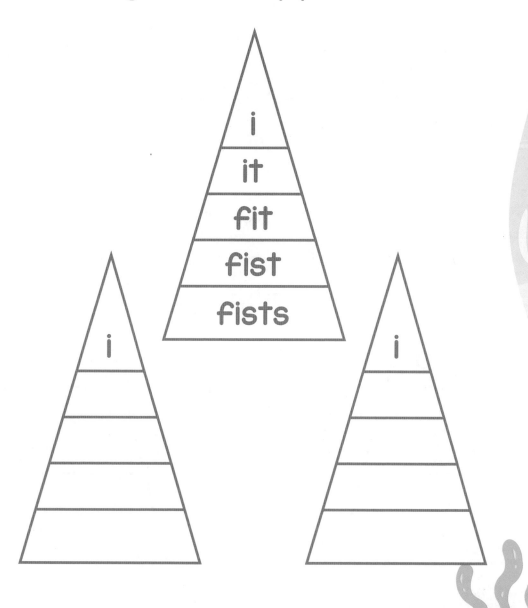

Word Pyramid

The vowel 'o'

Building a 3-level pyramid

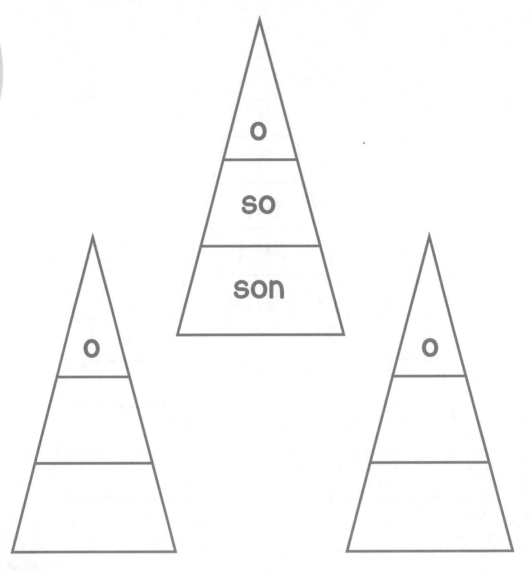

o

so

son

o

o

130

The vowel 'o'
Building a 4-level pyramid

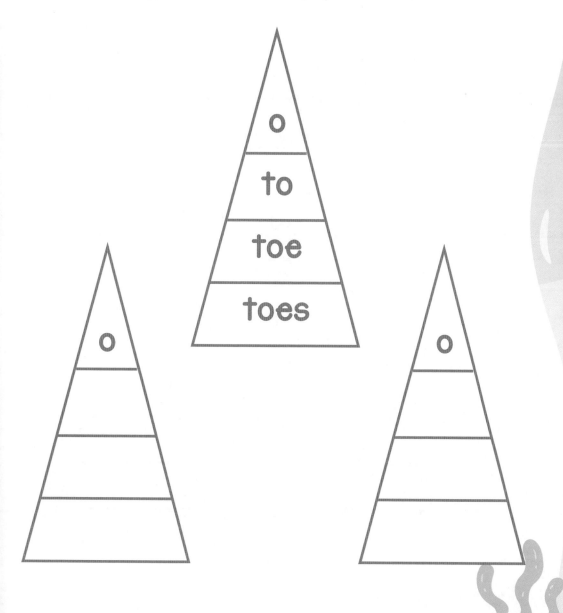

Word Pyramid

The vowel 'o'

Building a 5-level pyramid

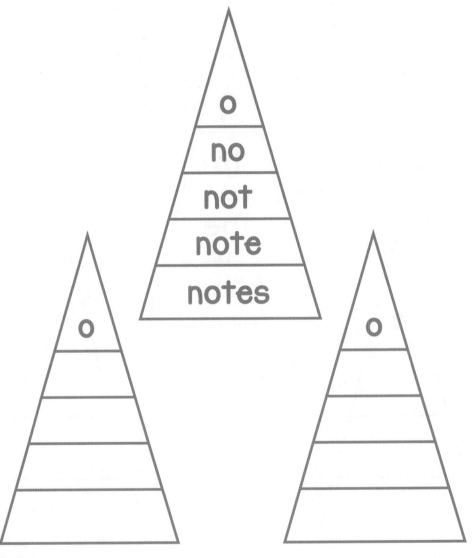

o

no

not

note

notes

o

o

132

The vowel 'u'
Building a 3-level pyramid

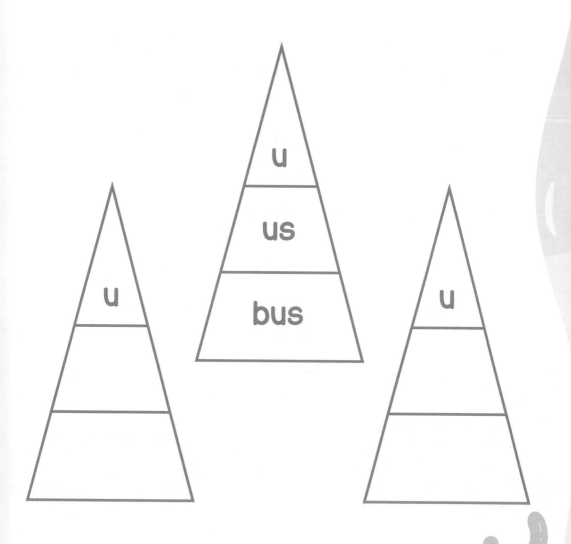

Word Pyramid

The vowel 'u'

Building a 4-level pyramid

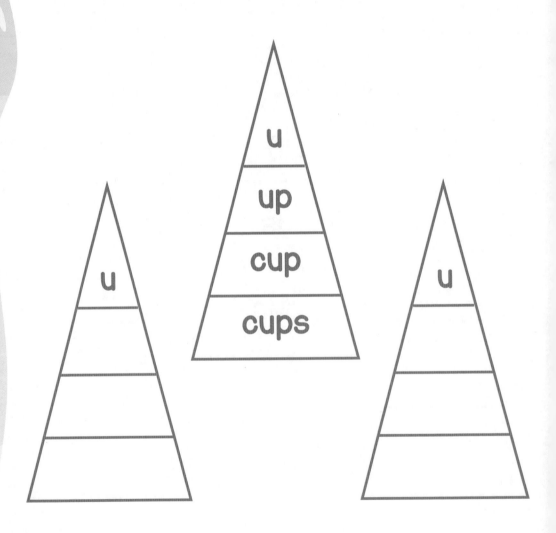

u

up

cup

cups

u

u

134

The vowel 'u'
Building a 5-level pyramid

Word Pyramid

Challenges!

Building 6-level pyramids with the vowels 'a, e, i, o, u'

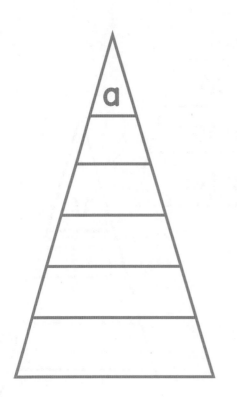

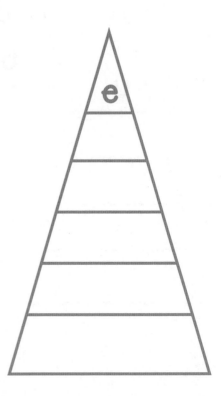

136

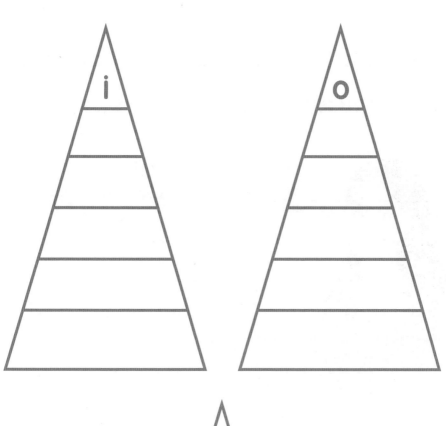

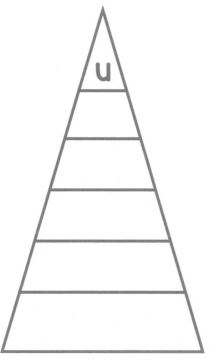

137

Well done, students! You can check your answers with the Answer Key.

Answer Key

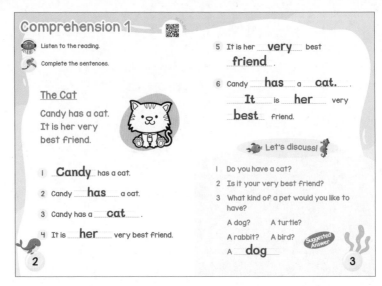

Comprehension 1

Listen to the reading.

Complete the sentences.

The Cat

Candy has a cat.
It is her very
best friend.

1 __Candy__ has a cat.

2 Candy __has__ a cat.

3 Candy has a __cat__ .

4 It is __her__ very best friend.

5 It is her __very__ best
__friend__ .

6 Candy __has__ a __cat.__ .
__It__ is __her__ very
__best__ friend.

Let's discuss!

1 Do you have a cat?

2 Is it your very best friend?

3 What kind of a pet would you like to have?

A dog?   A turtle?

A rabbit? A bird?

A __dog__

Suggested Answer

2   3

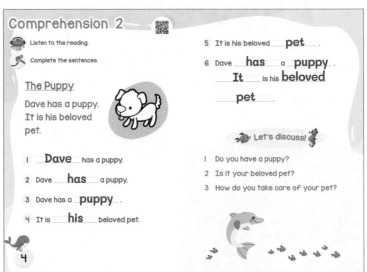

Comprehension 2

Listen to the reading.

Complete the sentences.

The Puppy

Dave has a puppy.
It is his beloved
pet.

1 __Dave__ has a puppy.

2 Dave __has__ a puppy.

3 Dave has a __puppy__ .

4 It is __his__ beloved pet.

5 It is his beloved __pet__ .

6 Dave __has__ a __puppy__ .
__It__ is his __beloved__
__pet__ .

Let's discuss!

1 Do you have a puppy?

2 Is it your beloved pet?

3 How do you take care of your pet?

4

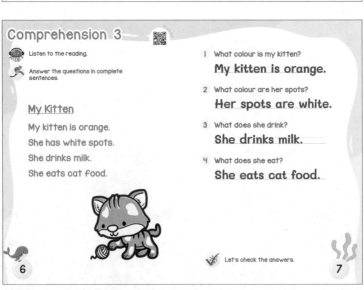

Comprehension 3

Listen to the reading.

Answer the questions in complete sentences.

My Kitten

My kitten is orange.
She has white spots.
She drinks milk.
She eats cat food.

1 What colour is my kitten?
My kitten is orange.

2 What colour are her spots?
Her spots are white.

3 What does she drink?
She drinks milk.

4 What does she eat?
She eats cat food.

Let's check the answers.

6   7

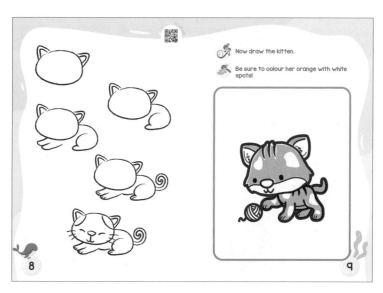

Now draw the kitten.

Be sure to colour her orange with white spots!

Comprehension 4

Listen to the reading.

Answer the questions in complete sentences.

The Duck

Here is a white duck.
Her beak is yellow.
She likes to swim.
She lives in the pond.

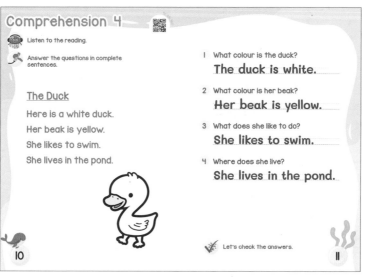

1 What colour is the duck?
   The duck is white.

2 What colour is her beak?
   Her beak is yellow.

3 What does she like to do?
   She likes to swim.

4 Where does she live?
   She lives in the pond.

Let's check the answers.

Let's think!

Where can you see ducks in Hong Kong?

In the parks?

Now draw two ducks swimming in the pond.

Colour the picture.

Suggested Answer

141

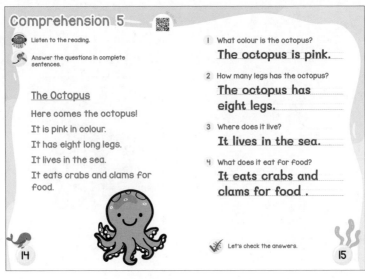

Comprehension 5

Listen to the reading.

Answer the questions in complete sentences.

The Octopus

Here comes the octopus!
It is pink in colour.
It has eight long legs.
It lives in the sea.
It eats crabs and clams for food.

1 What colour is the octopus?
The octopus is pink.

2 How many legs has the octopus?
The octopus has eight legs.

3 Where does it live?
It lives in the sea.

4 What does it eat for food?
It eats crabs and clams for food .

Let's check the answers.

14   15

Draw an octopus swimming in the sea.

Colour the picture.

Suggested Answer

16   17

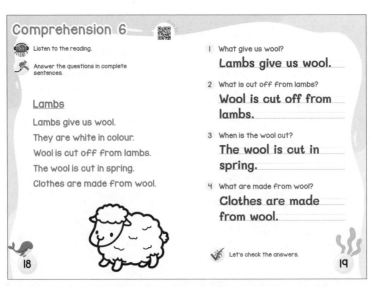

Comprehension 6

Listen to the reading.

Answer the questions in complete sentences.

Lambs

Lambs give us wool.
They are white in colour.
Wool is cut off from lambs.
The wool is cut in spring.
Clothes are made from wool.

1 What give us wool?
Lambs give us wool.

2 What is cut off from lambs?
Wool is cut off from lambs.

3 When is the wool cut?
The wool is cut in spring.

4 What are made from wool?
Clothes are made from wool.

Let's check the answers.

18   19

Let's think!

Why do we cut the lambs' wool in spring?

Why not in winter?

Now draw two lambs. One has its wool cut off!

Colour the picture.

Suggested Answer

20

21

Comprehension 7

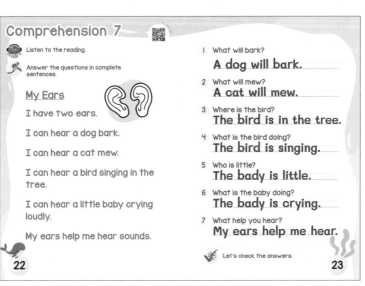

Listen to the reading.

Answer the questions in complete sentences.

My Ears

I have two ears.

I can hear a dog bark.

I can hear a cat mew.

I can hear a bird singing in the tree.

I can hear a little baby crying loudly.

My ears help me hear sounds.

1 What will bark?
   A dog will bark.

2 What will mew?
   A cat will mew.

3 Where is the bird?
   The bird is in the tree.

4 What is the bird doing?
   The bird is singing.

5 Who is little?
   The bady is little.

6 What is the baby doing?
   The bady is crying.

7 What help you hear?
   My ears help me hear.

Let's check the answers.

22

23

Comprehension 8
Using your Senses

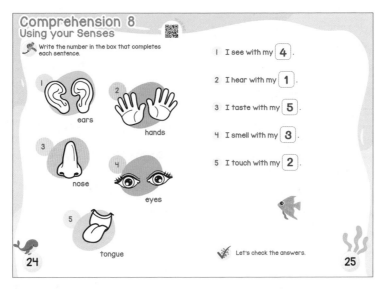

Write the number in the box that completes each sentence.

1. ears
2. hands
3. nose
4. eyes
5. tongue

1 I see with my [4].

2 I hear with my [1].

3 I taste with my [5].

4 I smell with my [3].

5 I touch with my [2].

Let's check the answers.

24

25

143

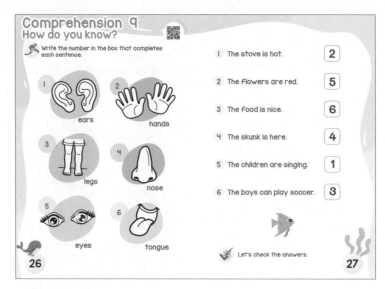

Comprehension 9
How do you know?

Write the number in the box that completes each sentence.

1. ears
2. hands
3. legs
4. nose
5. eyes
6. tongue

1 The stove is hot. **2**

2 The flowers are red. **5**

3 The food is nice. **6**

4 The skunk is here. **4**

5 The children are singing. **1**

6 The boys can play soccer. **3**

Let's check the answers.

26   27

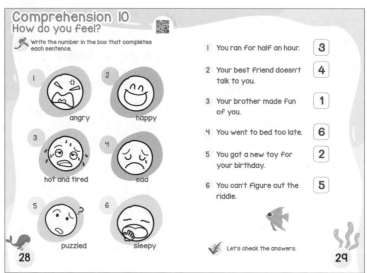

Comprehension 10
How do you feel?

Write the number in the box that completes each sentence.

1. angry
2. happy
3. hot and tired
4. sad
5. puzzled
6. sleepy

1 You ran for half an hour. **3**

2 Your best friend doesn't talk to you. **4**

3 Your brother made fun of you. **1**

4 You went to bed too late. **6**

5 You got a new toy for your birthday. **2**

6 You can't figure out the riddle. **5**

Let's check the answers.

28   29

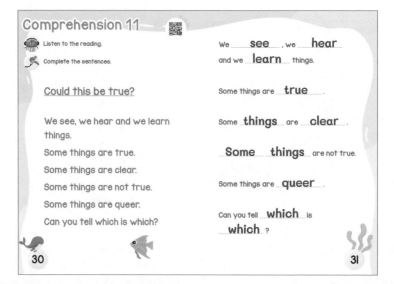

Comprehension 11

Listen to the reading.

Complete the sentences.

Could this be true?

We see, we hear and we learn things.
Some things are true.
Some things are clear.
Some things are not true.
Some things are queer.
Can you tell which is which?

We **see** , we **hear** and we **learn** things.

Some things are **true** .

Some **things** are **clear** .

Some things are not true.

Some things are **queer** .

Can you tell **which** is **which** ?

30   31

144

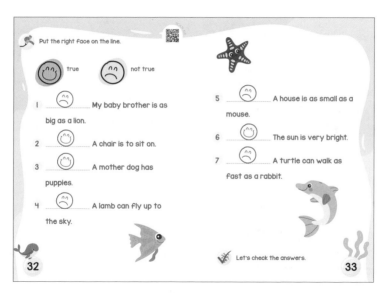

Put the right face on the line.

☺ true   ☹ not true

1 ____ My baby brother is as big as a lion.

2 ____ A chair is to sit on.

3 ____ A mother dog has puppies.

4 ____ A lamb can fly up to the sky.

5 ____ A house is as small as a mouse.

6 ____ The sun is very bright.

7 ____ A turtle can walk as fast as a rabbit.

Let's check the answers.

32

33

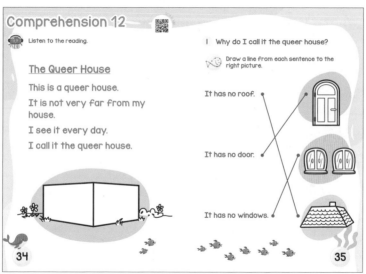

Comprehension 12

Listen to the reading.

The Queer House

This is a queer house.
It is not very far from my house.
I see it every day.
I call it the queer house.

1 Why do I call it the queer house?

Draw a line from each sentence to the right picture.

It has no roof.

It has no door.

It has no windows.

34

35

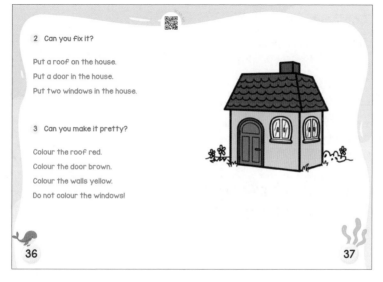

2 Can you fix it?

Put a roof on the house.
Put a door in the house.
Put two windows in the house.

3 Can you make it pretty?

Colour the roof red.
Colour the door brown.
Colour the walls yellow.
Do not colour the windows!

36

37

145

Comprehension 13

Say the names of the animals after me.

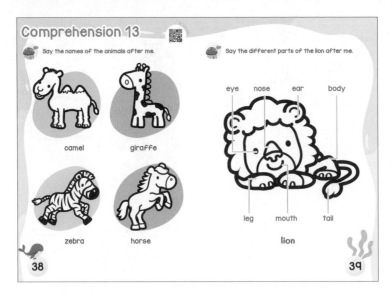

camel

giraffe

zebra

horse

Say the different parts of the lion after me.

eye   nose   ear   body

leg   mouth   tail

lion

38

39

What's this?

Look at the picture and guess what the part of the body belongs to.

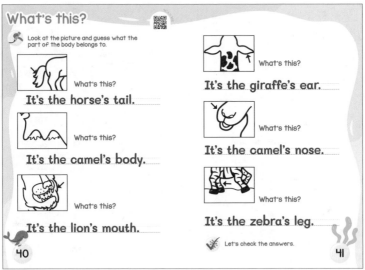

What's this?

It's the horse's tail.

What's this?

It's the camel's body.

What's this?

It's the lion's mouth.

What's this?

It's the giraffe's ear.

What's this?

It's the camel's nose.

What's this?

It's the zebra's leg.

Let's check the answers.

40

41

Comprehension 14

Have you got a good memory?

Look carefully at the picture. Try to remember everything.

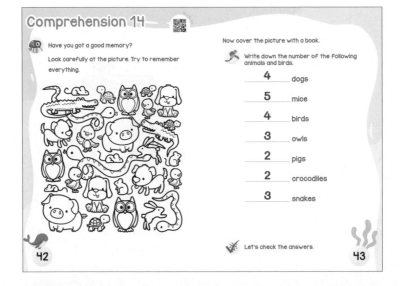

Now cover the picture with a book.

Write down the number of the following animals and birds.

4	dogs
5	mice
4	birds
3	owls
2	pigs
2	crocodiles
3	snakes

Let's check the answers.

146

42

43

Tongue Twisters
's' and 'f'

Look at the pictures and read the tongue twisters after me.

Underline all the words with the beginning sound 's' in number 1 and all the words with the beginning sound 'f' in number 2.

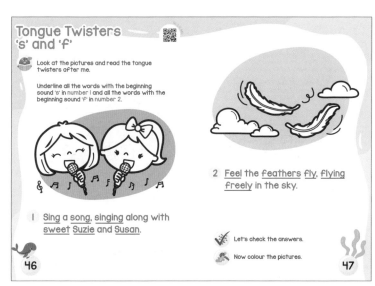

2 Feel the <u>feathers</u> <u>fly</u>, <u>flying</u> <u>freely</u> in the sky.

1 <u>Sing</u> a <u>song</u>, <u>singing</u> along with <u>sweet</u> <u>Suzie</u> and <u>Susan</u>.

Let's check the answers.

Now colour the pictures.

46

47

Tongue Twisters
'h' and 't'

Look at the pictures and read the tongue twisters after me.

Underline all the words with the beginning sound 'h' in number 3 and all the words with the beginning sound 't' in number 4.

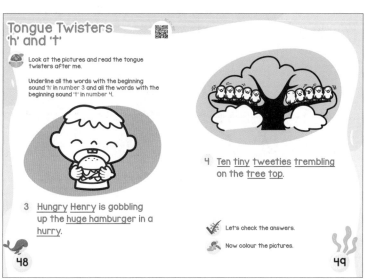

4 <u>Ten</u> <u>tiny</u> <u>tweeties</u> <u>trembling</u> on the <u>tree</u> <u>top</u>.

3 <u>Hungry</u> <u>Henry</u> is gobbling up the <u>huge</u> <u>hamburger</u> in a <u>hurry</u>.

Let's check the answers.

Now colour the pictures.

48

49

Tongue Twisters
'p' and 'm'

Look at the pictures and read the tongue twisters after me.

Underline all the words with the beginning sound 'p' in number 5 and all the words with the beginning sound 'm' in number 6.

6 <u>Mummy</u> is <u>making</u> <u>many</u> <u>muffins</u> for <u>Mable</u> and <u>Mark</u>.

5 <u>Polly</u> and <u>Patty</u> are <u>playing</u> with their <u>pretty</u> <u>puffy</u> <u>pet</u>.

Let's check the answers.

Now colour the pictures.

50

51

147

Tongue Twisters
'n' and 'r'

Look at the pictures and read the tongue twisters after me.

Underline all the words with the beginning sound 'n' in number 7 and all the words with the beginning sound 'r' in number 8.

7 Naughty Nick is jumping on Nelly's nice neat bed.

8 Row, row, rowing the red boat in the rain.

Let's check the answers.

Now colour the pictures.

52

53

Tongue Twisters
'b' and 'c'

Look at the pictures and read the tongue twisters after me.

Underline all the words with the beginning sound 'b' in number 9 and all the words with the beginning sound 'c' in number 10.

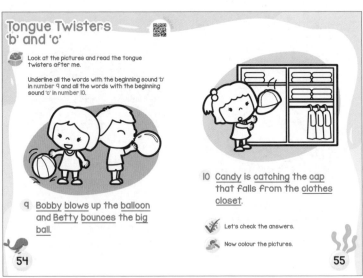

9 Bobby blows up the balloon and Betty bounces the big ball.

10 Candy is catching the cap that falls from the clothes closet.

Let's check the answers.

Now colour the pictures.

54

55

Tongue Twisters
'd' and 'l'

Look at the pictures and read the tongue twisters after me.

Underline all the words with the beginning sound 'd' in number 11 and all the words with the beginning sound 'l' in number 12.

11 Daddy is beating the drum while Daisy is dancing with the doggie.

12 Little Lily loves to lie lazily on the laptop.

Let's check the answers.

Now colour the pictures.

56

57

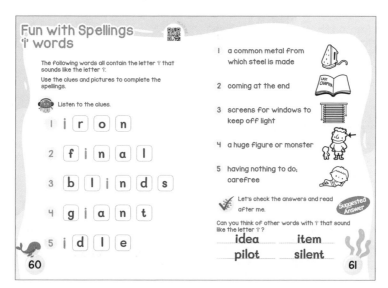

Fun with Spellings
'i' words

The following words all contain the letter 'i' that sounds like the letter 'i'.

Use the clues and pictures to complete the spellings.

Listen to the clues.

1. i r o n
2. f i n a l
3. b l i n d s
4. g i a n t
5. i d l e

1. a common metal from which steel is made
2. coming at the end
3. screens for windows to keep off light
4. a huge figure or monster
5. having nothing to do; carefree

Let's check the answers and read after me.

Can you think of other words with 'i' that sound like the letter 'i'?

idea item
pilot silent

60 | 61

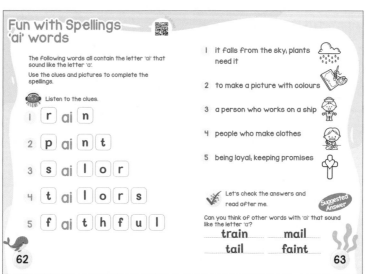

Fun with Spellings
'ai' words

The following words all contain the letter 'ai' that sound like the letter 'a'.

Use the clues and pictures to complete the spellings.

Listen to the clues.

1. r ai n
2. p ai n t
3. s ai l o r
4. t ai l o r s
5. f ai t h f u l

1. it falls from the sky; plants need it
2. to make a picture with colours
3. a person who works on a ship
4. people who make clothes
5. being loyal; keeping promises

Let's check the answers and read after me.

Can you think of other words with 'ai' that sound like the letter 'a'?

train mail
tail faint

62 | 63

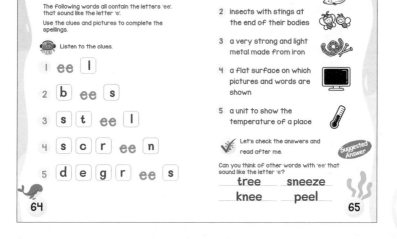

Fun with Spellings
'ee' words

The following words all contain the letters 'ee' that sound like the letter 'e'.

Use the clues and pictures to complete the spellings.

Listen to the clues.

1. ee l
2. b ee s
3. s t ee l
4. s c r ee n
5. d e g r ee s

1. a snake-like fish
2. insects with stings at the end of their bodies
3. a very strong and light metal made from iron
4. a flat surface on which pictures and words are shown
5. a unit to show the temperature of a place

Let's check the answers and read after me.

Can you think of other words with 'ee' that sound like the letter 'e'?

tree sneeze
knee peel

64 | 65

149

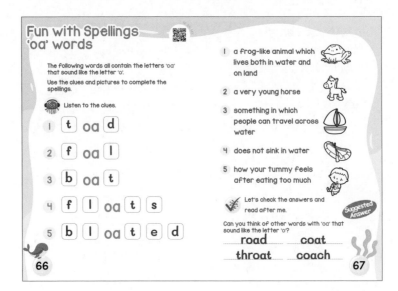

Fun with Spellings
'oa' words

The following words all contain the letters 'oa' that sound like the letter 'o'.

Use the clues and pictures to complete the spellings.

Listen to the clues.

1. t **oa** d
2. f **oa** l
3. b **oa** t
4. f l **oa** t s
5. b l **oa** t e d

1. a frog-like animal which lives both in water and on land
2. a very young horse
3. something in which people can travel across water
4. does not sink in water
5. how your tummy feels after eating too much

Let's check the answers and read after me.

Can you think of other words with 'oa' that sound like the letter 'o'?

road   coat
throat   coach

66   67

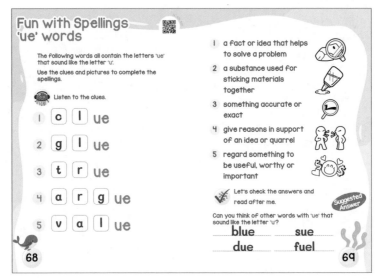

Fun with Spellings
'ue' words

The following words all contain the letters 'ue' that sound like the letter 'u'.

Use the clues and pictures to complete the spellings.

Listen to the clues.

1. c l ue
2. g l ue
3. t r ue
4. a r g ue
5. v a l ue

1. a fact or idea that helps to solve a problem
2. a substance used for sticking materials together
3. something accurate or exact
4. give reasons in support of an idea or quarrel
5. regard something to be useful, worthy or important

Let's check the answers and read after me.

Can you think of other words with 'ue' that sound like the letter 'u'?

blue   sue
due   fuel

68   69

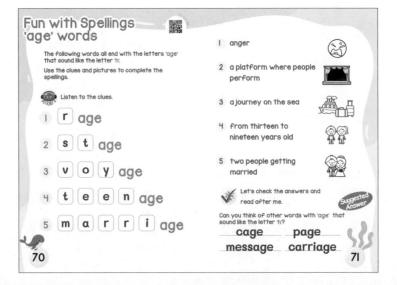

Fun with Spellings
'age' words

The following words all end with the letters 'age' that sound like the letter 'h'.

Use the clues and pictures to complete the spellings.

Listen to the clues.

1. r age
2. s t age
3. v o y age
4. t e e n age
5. m a r r i age

1. anger
2. a platform where people perform
3. a journey on the sea
4. from thirteen to nineteen years old
5. two people getting married

Let's check the answers and read after me.

Can you think of other words with 'age' that sound like the letter 'h'?

cage   page
message   carriage

70   71

150

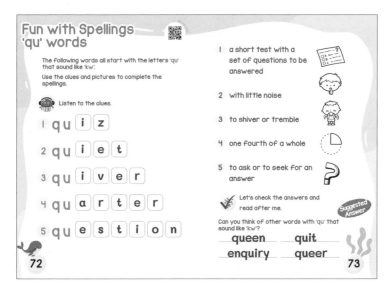

Fun with Spellings
'qu' words

The following words all start with the letters 'qu' that sound like 'kw'.

Use the clues and pictures to complete the spellings.

Listen to the clues.

1 qu i z
2 qu i e t
3 qu i v e r
4 qu a r t e r
5 qu e s t i o n

1 a short test with a set of questions to be answered

2 with little noise

3 to shiver or tremble

4 one fourth of a whole

5 to ask or to seek for an answer

Let's check the answers and read after me.

Suggested Answer

Can you think of other words with 'qu' that sound like 'kw'?

queen   **quit**
enquiry   **queer**

72   73

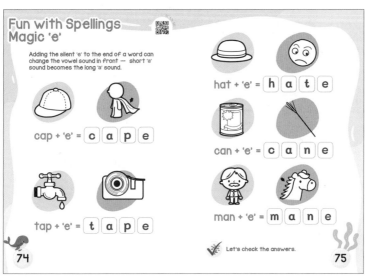

Fun with Spellings
Magic 'e'

Adding the silent 'e' to the end of a word can change the vowel sound in front — short 'a' sound becomes the long 'a' sound.

cap + 'e' = c a p e

tap + 'e' = t a p e

hat + 'e' = h a t e

can + 'e' = c a n e

man + 'e' = m a n e

Let's check the answers.

74   75

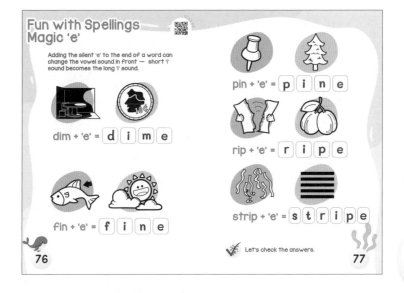

Fun with Spellings
Magic 'e'

Adding the silent 'e' to the end of a word can change the vowel sound in front — short 'i' sound becomes the long 'i' sound.

dim + 'e' = d i m e

fin + 'e' = f i n e

pin + 'e' = p i n e

rip + 'e' = r i p e

strip + 'e' = s t r i p e

Let's check the answers.

76   77

151

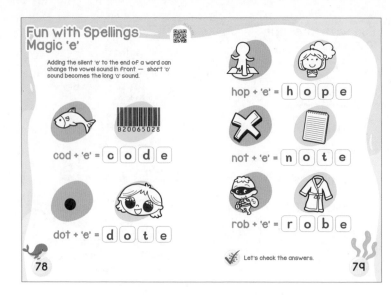

Fun with Spellings
Magic 'e'

Adding the silent 'e' to the end of a word can change the vowel sound in front — short 'o' sound becomes the long 'o' sound.

cod + 'e' = c o d e

dot + 'e' = d o t e

hop + 'e' = h o p e

not + 'e' = n o t e

rob + 'e' = r o b e

B20065028

Let's check the answers.

78   79

Fun with Spellings
Magic 'e'

Adding the silent 'e' to the end of a word can change the vowel sound in front — short 'u' sound becomes the long 'u' sound.

cut + 'e' = c u t e

tub + 'e' = t u b e

run + 'e' = r u n e

dun + 'e' = d u n e

Let's check the answers.

80   81

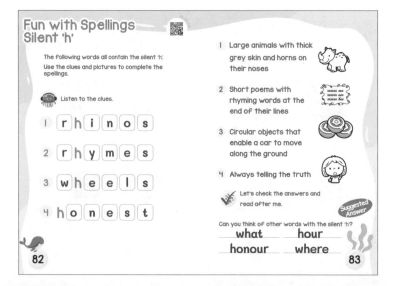

Fun with Spellings
Silent 'h'

The following words all contain the silent 'h'.
Use the clues and pictures to complete the spellings.

Listen to the clues.

1 r h i n o s

2 r h y m e s

3 w h e e l s

4 h o n e s t

1 Large animals with thick grey skin and horns on their noses

2 Short poems with rhyming words at the end of their lines

3 Circular objects that enable a car to move along the ground

4 Always telling the truth

Let's check the answers and read after me.

Suggested Answer

Can you think of other words with the silent 'h'?

<u>what</u>   <u>hour</u>
<u>honour</u>   <u>where</u>

82   83

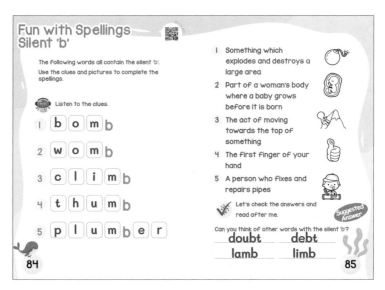

Fun with Spellings
Silent 'b'

The following words all contain the silent 'b'.
Use the clues and pictures to complete the spellings.

Listen to the clues.

1. b o m b
2. w o m b
3. c l i m b
4. t h u m b
5. p l u m b e r

1. Something which explodes and destroys a large area
2. Part of a woman's body where a baby grows before it is born
3. The act of moving towards the top of something
4. The first finger of your hand
5. A person who fixes and repairs pipes

Let's check the answers and read after me.

Suggested Answer

Can you think of other words with the silent 'b'?

doubt   debt
lamb   limb

84
85

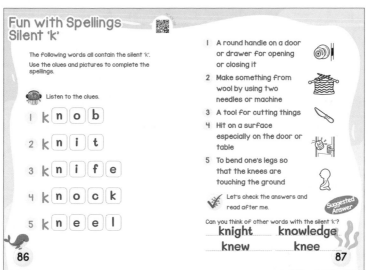

Fun with Spellings
Silent 'k'

The following words all contain the silent 'k'.
Use the clues and pictures to complete the spellings.

Listen to the clues.

1. k n o b
2. k n i t
3. k n i f e
4. k n o c k
5. k n e e l

1. A round handle on a door or drawer for opening or closing it
2. Make something from wool by using two needles or machine
3. A tool for cutting things
4. Hit on a surface especially on the door or table
5. To bend one's legs so that the knees are touching the ground

Let's check the answers and read after me.

Suggested Answer

Can you think of other words with the silent 'k'?

knight   knowledge
knew   knee

86
87

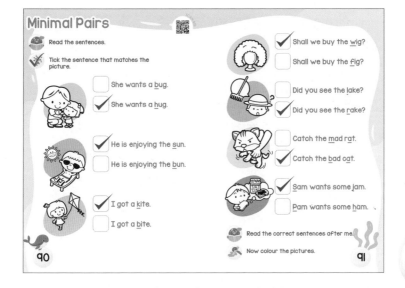

Minimal Pairs

Read the sentences.

Tick the sentence that matches the picture.

- [ ] She wants a bug.
- [x] She wants a hug.

- [x] He is enjoying the sun.
- [ ] He is enjoying the bun.

- [x] I got a kite.
- [ ] I got a bite.

- [x] Shall we buy the wig?
- [ ] Shall we buy the fig?

- [ ] Did you see the lake?
- [x] Did you see the rake?

- [ ] Catch the mad rat.
- [x] Catch the bad cat.

- [x] Sam wants some jam.
- [ ] Pam wants some ham.

Read the correct sentences after me.

Now colour the pictures.

90
91

153

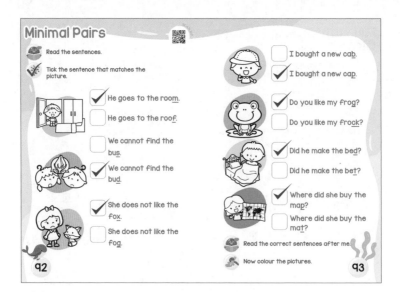

Minimal Pairs

Read the sentences.

Tick the sentence that matches the picture.

- ✓ He goes to the room.
- ☐ He goes to the roof.

- ☐ We cannot find the bus.
- ✓ We cannot find the bud.

- ✓ She does not like the fox.
- ☐ She does not like the fog.

92

- ☐ I bought a new cab.
- ✓ I bought a new cap.

- ✓ Do you like my frog?
- ☐ Do you like my frock?

- ✓ Did he make the bed?
- ☐ Did he make the bet?

- ✓ Where did she buy the map?
- ☐ Where did she buy the mat?

Read the correct sentences after me.

Now colour the pictures.

93

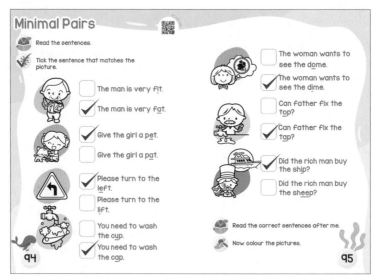

Minimal Pairs

Read the sentences.

Tick the sentence that matches the picture.

- ☐ The man is very fit.
- ✓ The man is very fat.

- ✓ Give the girl a pet.
- ☐ Give the girl a pat.

- ✓ Please turn to the left.
- ☐ Please turn to the lift.

- ☐ You need to wash the cup.
- ✓ You need to wash the cap.

94

- ☐ The woman wants to see the dome.
- ✓ The woman wants to see the dime.

- ☐ Can father fix the top?
- ✓ Can father fix the tap?

- ✓ Did the rich man buy the ship?
- ☐ Did the rich man buy the sheep?

Read the correct sentences after me.

Now colour the pictures.

95

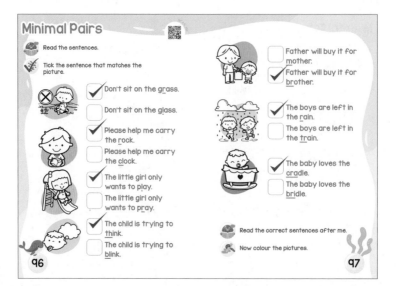

Minimal Pairs

Read the sentences.

Tick the sentence that matches the picture.

- ✓ Don't sit on the grass.
- ☐ Don't sit on the glass.

- ✓ Please help me carry the rock.
- ☐ Please help me carry the clock.

- ✓ The little girl only wants to play.
- ☐ The little girl only wants to pray.

- ✓ The child is trying to think.
- ☐ The child is trying to blink.

96

- ☐ Father will buy it for mother.
- ✓ Father will buy it for brother.

- ✓ The boys are left in the rain.
- ☐ The boys are left in the train.

- ✓ The baby loves the cradle.
- ☐ The baby loves the bridle.

Read the correct sentences after me.

Now colour the pictures.

97

154

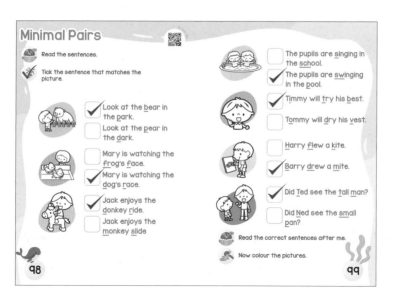

Minimal Pairs

Read the sentences.

Tick the sentence that matches the picture.

- ☑ Look at the <u>b</u>ear in the <u>p</u>ark.
- ☐ Look at the <u>p</u>ear in the <u>d</u>ark.

- ☐ Mary is watching the <u>fr</u>og's <u>f</u>ace.
- ☑ Mary is watching the <u>d</u>og's <u>r</u>ace.

- ☑ Jack enjoys the <u>d</u>onkey <u>r</u>ide.
- ☐ Jack enjoys the <u>m</u>onkey <u>sl</u>ide.

- ☐ The pupils are <u>s</u>inging in the <u>sch</u>ool.
- ☑ The pupils are <u>sw</u>inging in the <u>p</u>ool.

- ☑ Timmy will <u>tr</u>y his <u>b</u>est.
- ☐ Tommy will <u>dr</u>y his <u>v</u>est.

- ☐ <u>H</u>arry <u>fl</u>ew a <u>k</u>ite.
- ☑ <u>B</u>arry <u>dr</u>ew a <u>m</u>ite.

- ☑ Did <u>T</u>ed see the <u>t</u>all <u>m</u>an?
- ☐ Did <u>N</u>ed see the <u>sm</u>all <u>p</u>an?

Read the correct sentences after me.

Now colour the pictures.

98 | 99

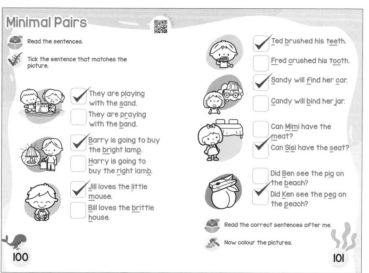

Minimal Pairs

Read the sentences.

Tick the sentence that matches the picture.

- ☑ They are <u>pl</u>aying with the <u>s</u>and.
- ☐ They are <u>pr</u>aying with the <u>b</u>and.

- ☑ <u>B</u>arry is going to buy the <u>br</u>ight <u>l</u>amp.
- ☐ <u>H</u>arry is going to buy the <u>r</u>ight <u>l</u>amb.

- ☑ <u>J</u>ill loves the <u>l</u>ittle <u>m</u>ouse.
- ☐ <u>B</u>ill loves the <u>br</u>ittle <u>h</u>ouse.

- ☑ <u>T</u>ed <u>br</u>ushed his <u>t</u>ee<u>th</u>.
- ☐ <u>Fr</u>ed <u>cr</u>ushed his <u>t</u>oo<u>th</u>.

- ☑ Sandy will <u>f</u>ind her <u>c</u>ar.
- ☐ Candy will <u>b</u>ind her <u>j</u>ar.

- ☐ Can <u>M</u>imi have the <u>m</u>eat?
- ☑ Can <u>S</u>isi have the <u>s</u>eat?

- ☐ Did <u>B</u>en see the <u>p</u>ig on the <u>b</u>each?
- ☑ Did <u>K</u>en see the <u>p</u>eg on the <u>p</u>each?

Read the correct sentences after me.

Now colour the pictures.

100 | 101

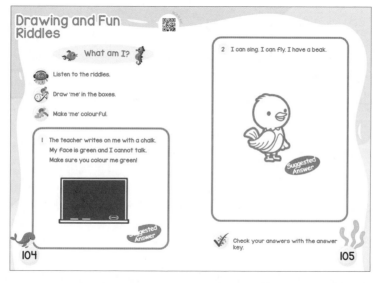

Drawing and Fun Riddles

What am I?

Listen to the riddles.

Draw 'me' in the boxes.

Make 'me' colourful.

1 The teacher writes on me with a chalk.
My face is green and I cannot talk.
Make sure you colour me green!

Suggested Answer

2 I can sing. I can fly. I have a beak.

Suggested Answer

Check your answers with the answer key.

104 | 105

What am I?

Listen to the riddles.

Draw 'me' in the boxes.

Make 'me' colourful.

3 My name sounds like the letter 'u'.
   I am an animal. Colour me white!

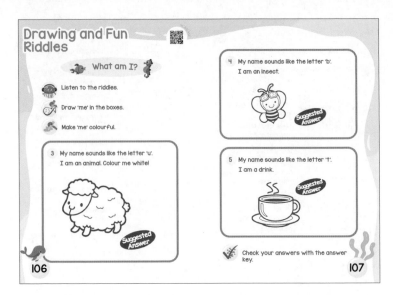

Suggested Answer

4 My name sounds like the letter 'b'.
   I am an insect.

Suggested Answer

5 My name sounds like the letter 't'.
   I am a drink.

Suggested Answer

Check your answers with the answer key.

106

107

What am I?

Listen to the riddles.

Draw 'me' in the boxes.

Make 'me' colourful.

6 My first letter is in 'sun' and also in 'set'.
   My second letter is both in 'lap' and 'top'.
   My third and fourth letters are twins in the 'pool'.
   My fifth letter is in the middle of the 'end'.

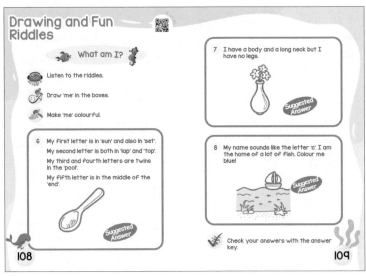

Suggested Answer

7 I have a body and a long neck but I have no legs.

Suggested Answer

8 My name sounds like the letter 'c'. I am the home of a lot of fish. Colour me blue!

Suggested Answer

Check your answers with the answer key.

108

109

What am I?

Listen to the riddle.

Draw 'me' in the box.

Make 'me' colourful.

9 My first letter begins in my 'hair'.
   My second letter is silent in my 'toe'.
   My third letter is in the middle of my 'heart' and 'ear'.
   My fourth letter is at the end of my 'hand'.

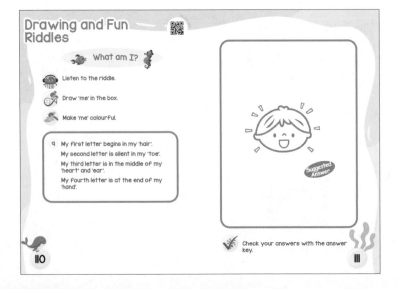

Suggested Answer

Check your answers with the answer key.

110

111

1 Which months have twenty-eight days in them?

All the twelve months.

2 My aunt has a sister but this woman is not my aunt. Who is she?

My mother.

3 What do you add to a road to make it broad?

The letter 'b'.

4 What table has no legs?

A time-table/Vegetable.

5 What hands cannot carry things?

The hands of a clock.

6 It stands in the middle of 'water' and appears twice in a 'turtle'. What is it?

The letter 't'.

Let's check the answers.

114

115

Wrack your Brain!

7 There are two fathers and two sons. Each of them carries an umbrella but there are only three umbrellas. How can this be?

Only three persons are there — grandfather, father and son.

8 There are twelve legs in the chicken farm but there are only five chickens. How can it be?

Five chickens have ten legs, the other two legs belong to the farmer.

9 There are eight boys and a basket with eight eggs in it. Each boy has one egg but one egg remains in the basket. How can it be?

The last boy is holding the basket with the last egg in it.

10 If you spell the word 's-t-r-e-s-s-e-d' from the end to the beginning, then miracle happens: something unhappy becomes something very sweet. What is it?

d-e-s-s-e-r-t-s.

Let's check the answers.

116

117

Word Pyramid

It starts off with one letter.

Add a new letter to it every time you build a new level.

No letters can be taken away but their order can be changed.

The vowel 'a'

Building a 3-level pyramid

Suggested Answer

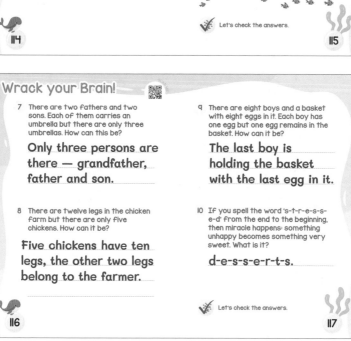

120

121

157

Word Pyramid

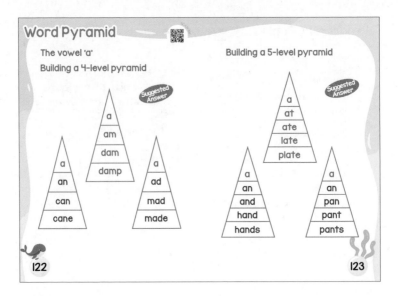

The vowel 'a'
Building a 4-level pyramid

Building a 5-level pyramid

Suggested Answer

| a |
| am |
| dam |
| damp |

| a |
| an |
| can |
| cane |

| a |
| ad |
| mad |
| made |

| a |
| at |
| ate |
| late |
| plate |

| a |
| an |
| and |
| hand |
| hands |

| a |
| an |
| pan |
| pant |
| pants |

122

123

Word Pyramid

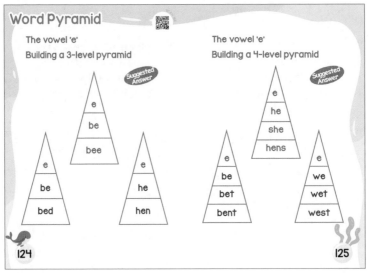

The vowel 'e'
Building a 3-level pyramid

The vowel 'e'
Building a 4-level pyramid

Suggested Answer

| e |
| be |
| bee |

| e |
| be |
| bed |

| e |
| he |
| hen |

| e |
| he |
| she |
| hens |

| e |
| be |
| bet |
| bent |

| e |
| we |
| wet |
| west |

124

125

Word Pyramid

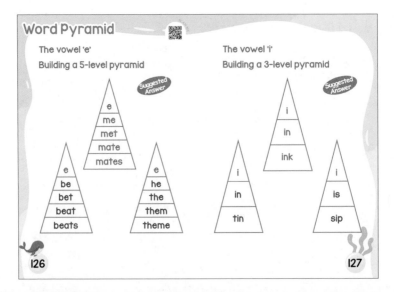

The vowel 'e'
Building a 5-level pyramid

The vowel 'i'
Building a 3-level pyramid

Suggested Answer

| e |
| me |
| met |
| mate |
| mates |

| e |
| be |
| bet |
| beat |
| beats |

| e |
| he |
| the |
| them |
| theme |

| i |
| in |
| ink |

| i |
| in |
| tin |

| i |
| is |
| sip |

126

127

158

Word Pyramid

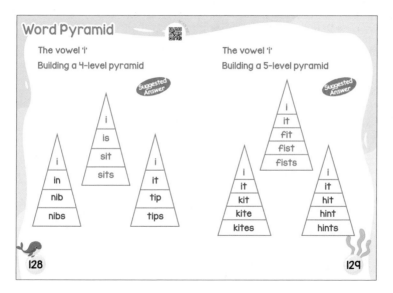

The vowel 'i'
Building a 4-level pyramid

Suggested Answer

i
is
sit
sits

i
in
nib
nibs

i
it
tip
tips

The vowel 'i'
Building a 5-level pyramid

Suggested Answer

i
it
fit
fist
fists

i
it
kit
kite
kites

i
it
hit
hint
hints

128

129

Word Pyramid

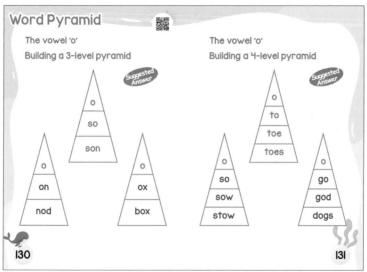

The vowel 'o'
Building a 3-level pyramid

Suggested Answer

o
so
son

o
on
nod

o
ox
box

The vowel 'o'
Building a 4-level pyramid

Suggested Answer

o
to
toe
toes

o
so
sow
stow

o
go
god
dogs

130

131

Word Pyramid

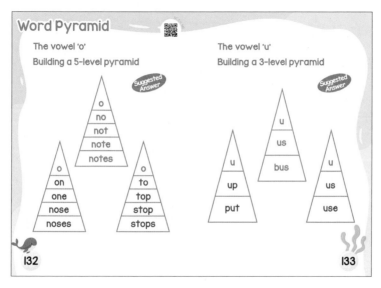

The vowel 'o'
Building a 5-level pyramid

Suggested Answer

o
no
not
note
notes

o
on
one
nose
noses

o
to
top
stop
stops

The vowel 'u'
Building a 3-level pyramid

Suggested Answer

u
us
bus

u
up
put

u
us
use

132

133

159

Word Pyramid

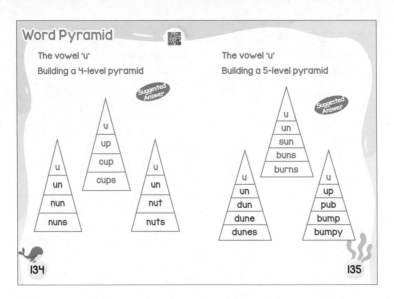

The vowel 'u'
Building a 4-level pyramid

The vowel 'u'
Building a 5-level pyramid

Suggested Answer

u
up
cup
cups

u
un
nun
nuns

u
un
nut
nuts

Suggested Answer

u
un
sun
buns
burns

u
un
dun
dune
dunes

u
up
pub
bump
bumpy

134

135

Word Pyramid

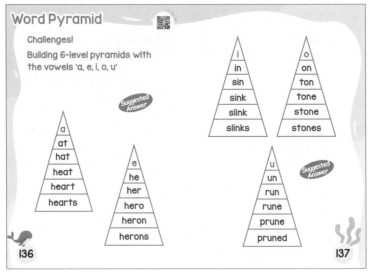

Challenges!
Building 6-level pyramids with
the vowels 'a, e, i, o, u'

Suggested Answer

a
at
hat
heat
heart
hearts

e
he
her
hero
heron
herons

i
in
sin
sink
slink
slinks

o
on
ton
tone
stone
stones

Suggested Answer

u
un
run
rune
prune
pruned

136

137